ANIMALS IN THEIR WORLD

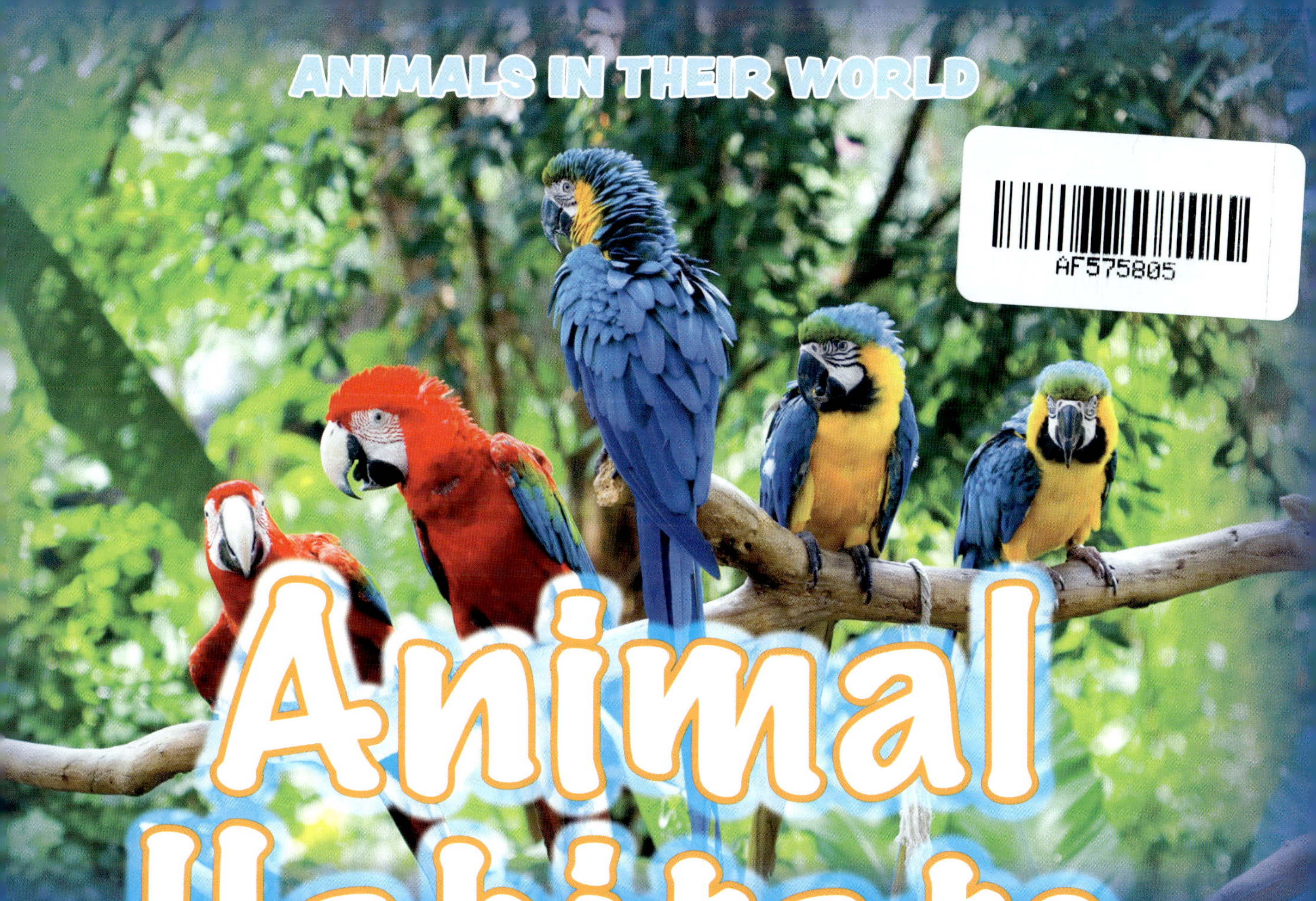

Animal Habitats

Christian Lopetz

A Crabtree Seedlings Book

Table of Contents

What Is a Habitat?

An animal's habitat is its home. A habitat contains all the things an animal needs to survive.

Animals need food, water, and shelter to survive.

Animals depend on other animals, plants, and their **environment** to live. This is called an **ecosystem**.

Desert Habitats

Many different animals make their habitats in the desert. A desert is a dry region with extreme temperatures and very little rain.

Who Lives Here?

Rattlesnakes hide in rocky crevices to stay cool. These are known as snake dens.

Cactus wrens make their nests inside cactuses. The prickly cactus spines protect the nest from **predators**.

Deserts usually get less than 10 inches (25 centimeters) of rain a year. Desert plants and animals must **adapt** to a harsh environment.

Scorpions have adapted to living in hot deserts by being **nocturnal**

Arctic Habitats

Not all deserts are hot. The Arctic is a cold, icy desert. It is located around the North Pole.

Who Lives Here?

Beluga whales live in the Arctic Ocean. They can survive the ocean's freezing temperatures because they have a thick layer of blubber.

Polar bears hunt and eat seals. Female polar bears make dens in the snow to give birth to cubs.

Arctic plants and animals must adapt to a harsh environment.

In winter, the Arctic fox has white fur that blends in with the snow. In summer it sheds its white coat for brown fur.

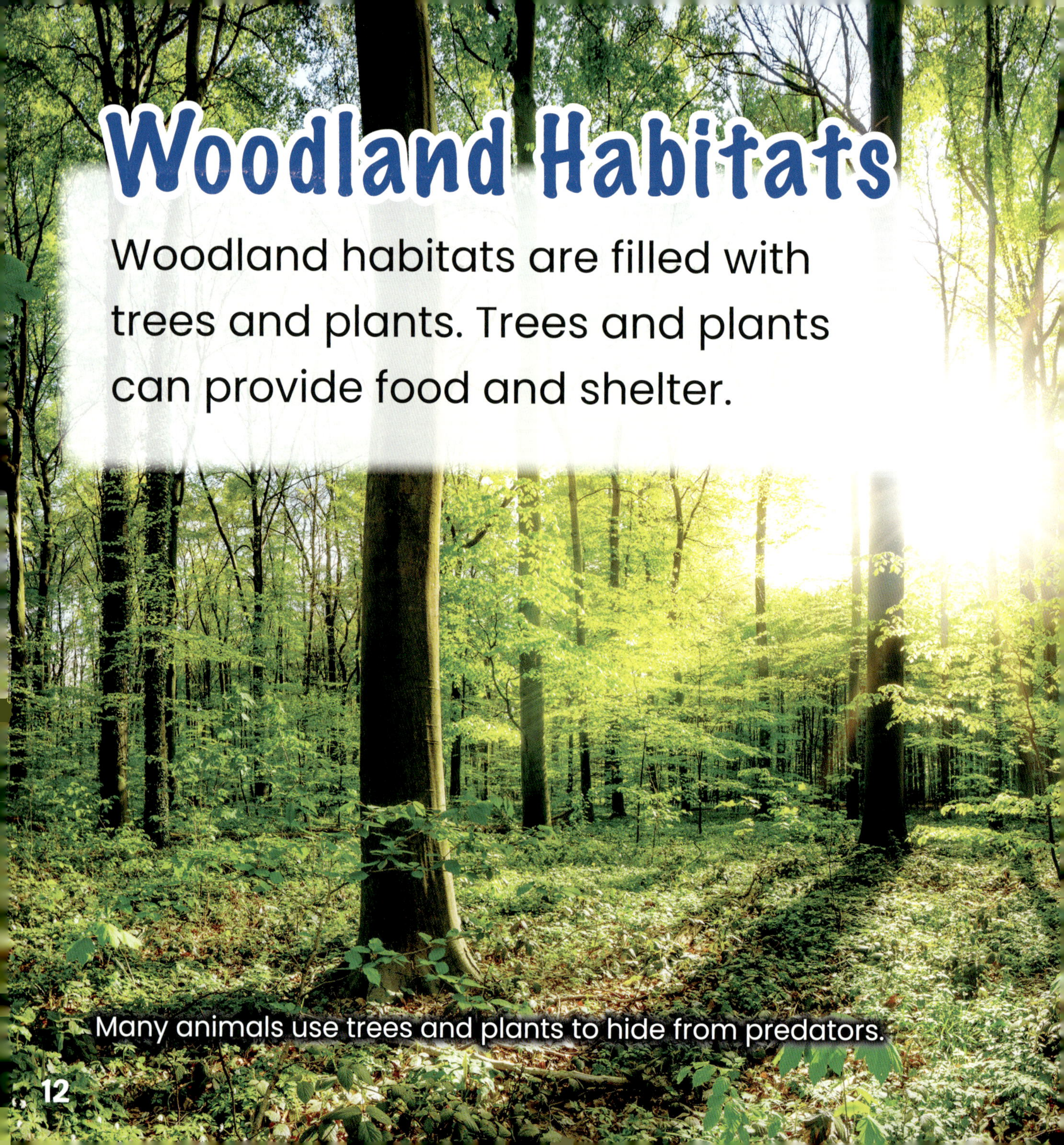

Woodland Habitats

Woodland habitats are filled with trees and plants. Trees and plants can provide food and shelter.

Many animals use trees and plants to hide from predators.

Who Lives Here?

Squirrels build nests in the woodland trees. They eat nuts, fruit, and seeds.

Great horned owls hunt many different animals, including raccoons and squirrels.

Raccoons make their dens in hollow trees or brush piles.

Rainforest Habitats

Tropical rain forests are warm and wet. Thousands of different kinds of plants and animals live in rain forests.

Who Lives Here?

Golden lion tamarins live in the **subcanopy** of the rain forest. They eat lizards, fruit, insects, and birds.

Poison dart frogs come in many different bright colors.Their bright colors warn predators to stay away.

Many rainforest animals lose their habitats because of **deforestation**.

Toucans nest in tree holes. They use their large, colorful beaks to reach fruit.

Freshwater Habitats

Most of the Earth is covered in water, but only one percent of it is **freshwater**. Freshwater habitats include ponds, lakes, rivers, and streams.

Who Lives Here?

Freshwater turtles climb onto rocks or logs to warm themselves in the Sun.

Bluegills live in ponds, lakes, and slow-moving streams. Male bluegills build nests for the female bluegills' eggs.

Egrets nest in trees near water and gather in groups called colonies. They eat fish, frogs, mice, and other small animals.

Ocean Habitats

About 70 percent of Earth's surface is covered in ocean water. Ocean water is salty.

Who Lives Here?

The octopus is recognized by its eight tentacles. An octopus can change the color of its skin to blend in with its surroundings.

The killer whale, also known as the Orca, lives in every ocean around the world, but is most common in Arctic and Antarctic waters.

Stingrays are fish. They prefer shallow, near-shore waters in warm parts of the world. They spend most of their time lying partially buried on the ocean floor.

Coral reefs are warm, shallow ocean habitats. Many ocean animals make their home in a coral reef.

Seahorses use their tails to anchor themselves to sea grasses and coral.

Glossary

adapt (uh-DAPT): To go through a change or changes to fit better in a certain environment

deforestation (de-FOR-ist-ay-shuhn): The cutting, clearing, and removal of forests

ecosystem (EE-koh-siss-tuhm): A community of plants and animals interacting with each other and the environment

environment (en-VYE-ruhn-muhnt): The surrounding natural world of land, water, and air

freshwater (FRESH-wa-tur): Water with no salt in it

nocturnal (nok-TUR-nuhl): To be active at night

predators (PRED-uh-turz): Animals that hunt and eat other animals

subcanopy (sub-CAN-uh-pee): A layer of trees that is below the canopy trees. Canopy trees cast shade on what grows below them.

tropical (TROP-uh-kuhl): Describes an area that is hot and rainy year-round

Index

It's our only home. Please keep Earth clean and safe for all living things.

School-to-Home Support for Caregivers and Teachers

This book helps children grow by letting them practice reading. Here are a few guiding questions to help the reader build his or her comprehension skills. Possible answers appear here in red.

Before Reading

- **What do I think this book is about?** I think this book is about all the different places animals live. I think this book is about how climate influences where some animals live.
- **What do I want to learn about this topic?** I want to learn more about animals and their varying habitats. I want to learn what animals need to survive around the world.

During Reading

- **I wonder why...** I wonder why the Arctic is considered a desert. I wonder why toucans have colorful beaks.
- **What have I learned so far?** I have learned that only 1% of the water that covers the Earth is freshwater. I have learned that about 70% of Earth's surface is covered in salty ocean water.

After Reading

- **What details did I learn about this topic?** I have learned that seahorses use their tails to anchor themselves to sea grasses and coral. I have learned that nocturnal means to be active at night.
- **Read the book again and look for the glossary words.** I see the word *ecosystem* on page 5, and the word *deforestation* on page 15. The other glossary words are found on page 22.

Library and Archives Canada Cataloguing in Publication

Available at the Library and Archives Canada

Library of Congress Cataloging-in-Publication Data

Available at the Library of Congress

Crabtree Publishing Company

www.crabtreebooks.com 1–800–387–7650

Print book version produced jointly with Blue Door Education in 2023

Written by: Christian Lopetz

Print coordinator: Katherine Berti

Printed in the U.S.A./072022/CG20220201

Photo Credits: istock.com, shutterstock.com, Cover ©Juriah Mosin; page 2-3 ©shutterstock.com/ Cavan-Images. page 4-5 © Peter Wollinga, SCOTTCHAN, inset pic ©Rich Carey. pages 6-7 © © Alexandr Vlassyuk, K13ART, You Touch Pix of EuToch. Page 8 desert © LHBLLC, scorpion © photosync ; page 9 and 10 Arctic landscape © Christopher Wood; map © Peter Hermes Furian. Page 10-11: polar bear ©Vaclav Sebek, Beluga Whale © Luna Vandoorne. Page 11 © NaturesMomentsuk (white fox), brown fox © shutterstock.com/Roxana Bashyrova. Page 12-13: © woodland landscape ©Guenter Albers. woodland animals © Steve Byland, Lori Labrecque, Ronnie Howard. Page 14-15 © Quick Shot Ralph Loesche, Toucan © buteo, dartfrog © worldswildlifewonders, golden tamarin © Edwin Butter, deforestation © Tarcisio Schnaider, Frontpage, Pages 16-17: © Jasper Suijten , Kokhanchikov, bluegill © Susan Ridley, turtle © Tim Maineiero, egret © FloridaStock. Pages 18-19: © Rich Carey, Tabooma, Kristina Vackova, CyberEak, Melissa King, Dmytro Tkachuk, Christian Musat, Thomas Neeser, EpicStockMedia; Pages 20-21: ©Rich Carey, Krzysztof Bargiel, Joe Belanger, Melissa King. Page 23: shutterstock.com/ Daniel Chetroni

Published in the United States
Crabtree Publishing
347 Fifth Ave.
Suite 1402-145
New York, NY 10016

Published in Canada
Crabtree Publishing
616 Welland Ave.
St. Catharines, Ontario
L2M 5V6